The Pig in the Pond

MARTIN WADDELL

ILLUSTRATED BY

JILL BARTON

WALKER BOOKS
AND SUBSIDIARIES

LONDON · BOSTON · SYDNEY · AUCKLAND

For Charlotte Maeve
M.W.

For Porky Boffin
J.B.

First published 1992 by Walker Books Ltd
87 Vauxhall Walk, London SE11 5HJ

This edition with CD published 2007

2 4 6 8 10 9 7 5 3 1

Text © 1992 Martin Waddell
Illustrations © 1992 Jill Barton

This book has been typeset in Veronan Light Educational

Printed in China

British Library Cataloguing in Publication Data:
a catalogue record for this book is available from the British Library

ISBN 978-1-4063-1097-9

www.walkerbooks.co.uk

This is the story of Neligan's pig.

One day Neligan went into town.
It was hot. It was dry.
The sun shone in the sky.
Neligan's pig sat by
Neligan's pond.

The ducks went, "Quack!"
The geese went, "Honk!"
They were cool on
the water in
Neligan's pond.

The pig sat in the sun.

She looked at the pond.

The ducks went, "Quack!"

The geese went, "Honk!"

The pig went, "Oink!"

She didn't go in,

because pigs don't swim.

The pig sat in the sun getting hotter and hotter.

The ducks went, "Quack, quack!"   The geese went, "Honk, honk!"

The pig went, "Oink, oink!" She didn't go in, because pigs don't swim.

The pig gulped and gasped and looked at the water.

The ducks went, "Quack, quack, quack!"

The geese went, "Honk, honk, honk!"

The pig went, "Oink, oink, oink!"

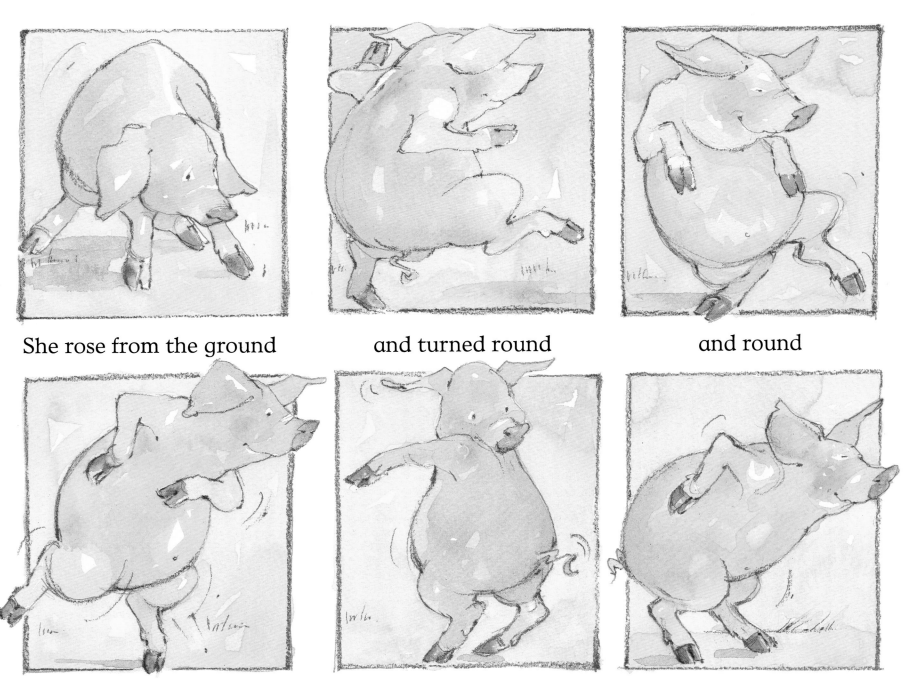

She rose from the ground

and turned round

and round

stamping her trotters

and twirling her tail

and. . .

SPLASH!

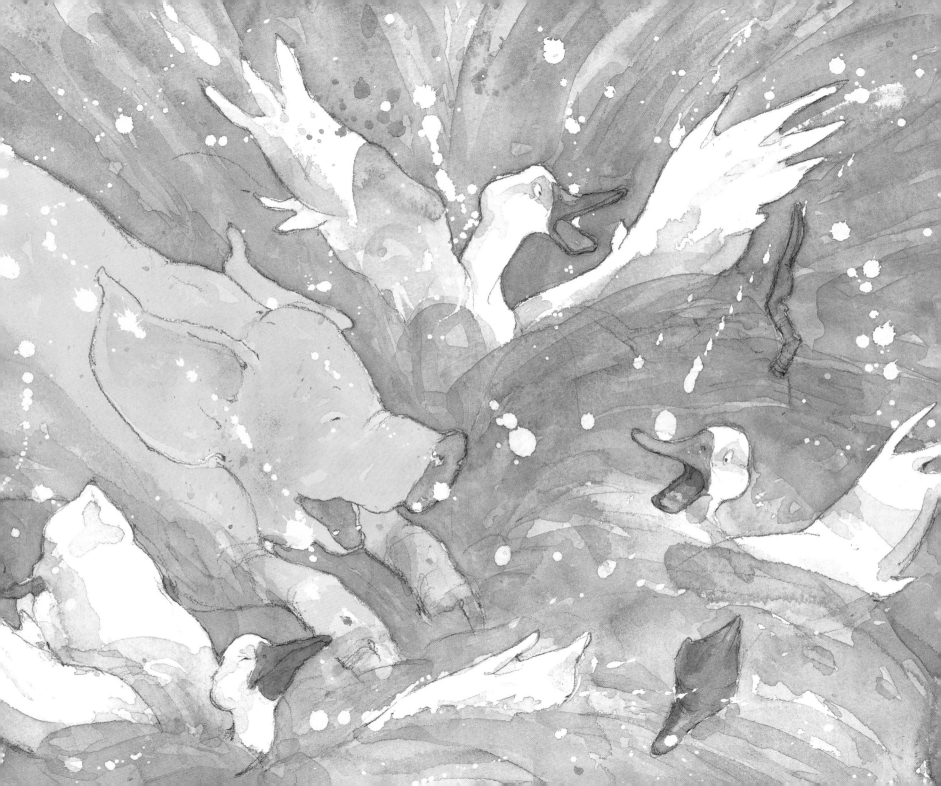

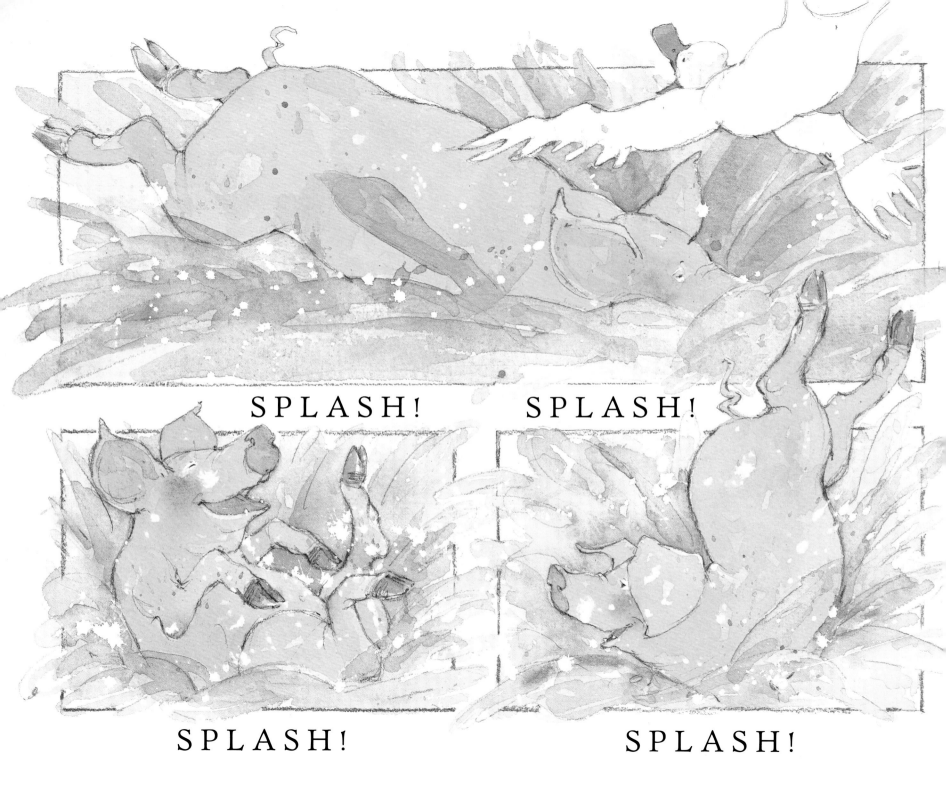

SPLASH! SPLASH!

SPLASH! SPLASH!

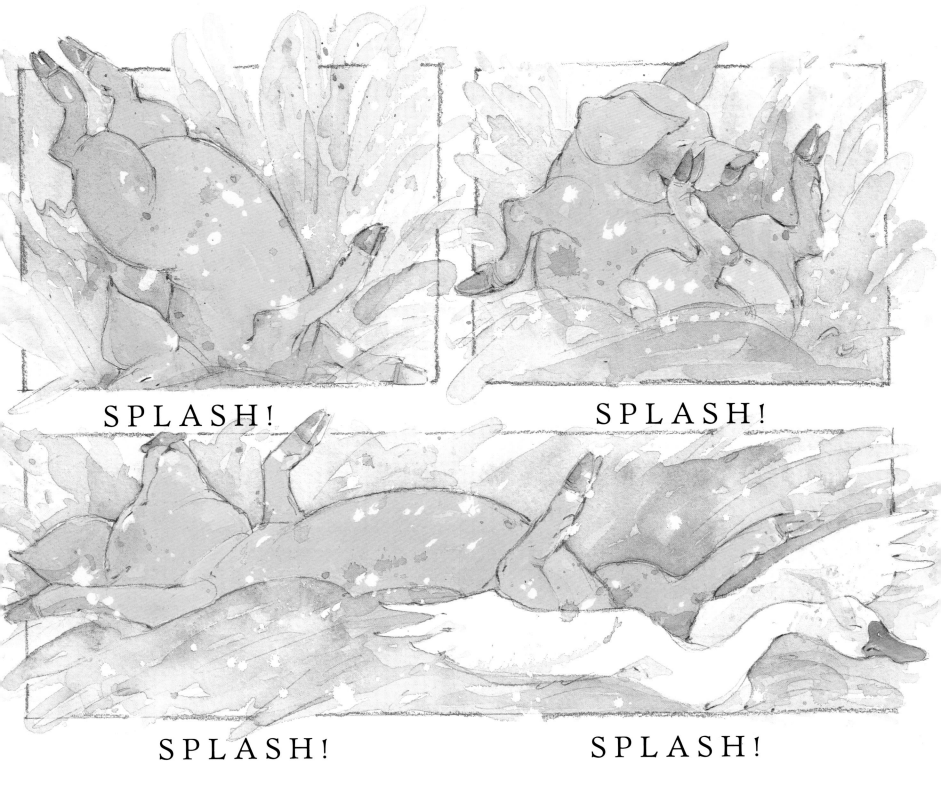

SPLASH!

SPLASH!

SPLASH!

SPLASH!

The ducks and the geese were splashed out of the pond.

The ducks went, "Quack, quack, quack, quack!"
The geese went, "Honk, honk, honk, honk!"
which means, very loudly, "The pig's in the pond!"

"The pig's in the pond!"

"The pig's in the pond!"

The word spread about, above and beyond,

"The pig's in the pond!"

"The pig's in the pond!"

"At Neligan's farm, the pig's in the pond!"

From the fields all around they came to see
the pig in the pond at Neligan's farm.
And then. . .

Neligan came on his cart!

Neligan looked at the pig in the pond.

The pig went, "Oink!"

Neligan took off his hat.

Neligan looked at the pig in the pond.

The pig went, "Oink, oink!"

Neligan took off his trousers and boots.

Neligan looked at the pig in the pond.

The pig went, "Oink, oink, oink!"

Neligan took off his shirt.

Neligan looked at the pig in the pond.

The pig went, "Oink, oink, oink, OINK!"

Neligan took off his pants and. . .

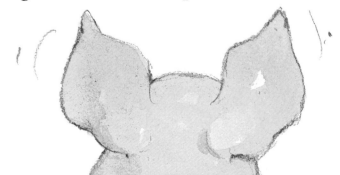

S P L A S H ! Neligan joined the pig in the pond.

What happened next?

SPLC

OOOOOOSH!

They all joined the pig in the pond!

And that was the story of Neligan's pig.